Mountains, Mists, Myths, and Murder

Clintonito Faraday Abrego, called Nito, Son of the famous Clint Faraday, head of Criminal Investigations (a silly title on the comarca Ngobe Bugle), Rep. de Panamá, is called by Moises Castillo Smith, chief of the Quebrada Tula area, to investigate the finding of two bodies near Misty Mountain. He becomes involved with an old myth of the people. Is that, in fact, behind the murders – or is it simply being used?

Contents

About the author

CD Moulton has traveled extensively over much of the world both in the music business, where he was a rock guitarist, songwriter and arranger and in an import/export business. He has been everything from a bar owner to auto salvage (junkyard) manager, longshoreman to high steel worker, orchid grower to landscaper, tropical fish farmer to commercial fisherman. He started writing books in 1983 and has published more than 350 books as of January 1, 2023. His most popular books to date are about research with orchids, though much of his science fiction and fantasy work has proven popular. He wrote the CD Grimes, PI series, and the Det. Nick Storie series, Clint Faraday series, and many other works.

He now resides in Gualaca, Chiriqui, Panamá, where he writes books, plays music with friends, does research with orchids and medicinal plants. He has lately become involved in fighting for the rights of the indigenous people, who are among his closest friends, and in fighting the extreme corruption in the courts and police in Panamá.

He offers the free e-book, *Fading Paradise*, that explains what he has been through because of the corruption.

CD is the discoverer of the Chadam Protocol for curing cancer.

Facebook page Ambrosia peruviana for cancer.

Mountains, Mists, Myths, and Murder

<u>*At Home in Paradise*</u>

Clintonito Faraday Abrego looked out over the Caribbean from his hammock on the front porch of the home his father and mother built 40 years ago and sighed contentedly. His 14 year old son, Guillermo, brought him a guayabana chicha and climbed into the hammock with him.

His father, the first Clint Faraday, had been a very famous detective, and was only the second non-indigeno person in history to be declared Ngobe. Clint was a detective, and Nito, as he was addressed, was the top graduate in his classes when he studied criminal investigation at the police academy. He was with the Policía Nacionál for 6 years before coming to the comarca, where he was requested by the council to be head of the police.

There was little for him to investigate in violent crimes, as the Ngobe are a very peaceful people, most of the time. As several presidents of Panamá had learned, they could also come together to oppose things that would harm the comarca and its people.

Nito's mother Tyna Abrego de Faraday, was pure Ngobe, and was the beauty on the comarca. She was 82 years old, and still a beauty. Nito was raised in the Ngobe tradition, and tended to the pragmatism of his father. None of the "Darling little prince" upbringing of the "outside" [anything not in the comarca] world. He had responsibilities since he was 6 years old. Before, actually. He was secure in his life, had a place in the community, and was empathetic with his people.

He was loved and wanted since before he was born. He had physical contact with his parents constantly for the first several years. He was taught self-discipline from day one, and his parents – or anyone else – had never hit him. When he did something"wrong" it was explained to him why it was wrong. He would never do anything to make his parents ashamed of his actions [never of him. Of things he had said or done].

The Ngobe are a touching people. It is part of the language. When you saw a friend you hadn't seen for awhile, you embraced, and it was a full body embrace, not a bending to touch at the shoulders.

Nito smiled, and Llermo [the last part of the

name is the nickname] asked him why, with a look.

"Like my Dad. I wonder what outsiders would think if they saw us together in this hammock."

"Why would they think anything? I don't get it!"

"They do not touch much. If they saw us, they would think it was about sex."

"With my father? That's stupid!"

"Any two males more than eight or nine years old, it would be the first thing they thought."

"Well, anyone but my own father, it could be, but why would they care? *They* aren't here doing anything."

"It's all in how they were raised. Sex is taboo until you're eighteen or twenty one or something."

"How stupid! I don't believe they don't know about sex when they're twelve or even ten. Nica fucked me when I was nine, but I already knew about it when I was a lot younger."

"He did?"

"He who ... oh. Nica. Sure."

"Did you like it?"

"Not much. I didn't get *my* rocks off. It wasn't bad, but I didn't like it."

Nito laughed. He remembered how his father and he would talk about sex. The difference was that Dad had admitted later that he was confused and even enraged, but had to act like a Gnobe and say, "Oh? Really? Did you like it?" when he really wanted to kill the one who screwed him.

He was like Llermo. He didn't like it, but just because he didn't like it. Not because it was evil or gay or whatever.

The saying was, "Some people like yuca, some like rice, some like both."

He had never understood how so many outsiders were so adamant about it. "Evil!" "Queer!"

The comarca recognized six sexes, and considered them all natural. Heterosexual male and female, bisexual male and female, homosexual male and female. Big deal. Pass the chicha. If a child was strictly gay or lesbian, they acted in certain ways at seven or eight years of age.

Most were bisexual, to one degree or another.

Why was he thinking of sex?

Because this was paradise, and you were who you were, not someone who someone else ordered what they felt and did. It was personal, not any of the community's business.

Of course, that was by consent. Force was never tolerated.

Double standard, too. Boys screwed each other and played with sex from the time they were eight years old. If you wanted something, you could seduce, but rape would get your head cut off with a dull machete. Girls, not until they were twelve. Period, and then only if they wanted it.

"Dad, I am having a big problem with the vainilla. None of the pollenation is taking. I think it's because of the water, but Yveth says it's the time of year, because the dawn is so bright. She says I have to get to it earlier."

"Yes. It only takes at sunrise, and the sun comes up fast this time of year. There's no mist or fog. Get to it just as soon as it's light enough to see, and before the sun is actually above the horizon."

"Oh. Okay.

"Yveth also says you'll have to go to Tula soon. I'd like to go, but she says it would be a bad idea, because it would make it dangerous for you and maybe me."

Yveth was the daughter of Matilde, the medicine woman in my father's time. She had some psy powers, and was never wrong about some things. Yveth was good, but she could be wrong.

"I will? Did she say why?"

"It's confused. It has something to do with the spirits on Misty Mountain."

"Misty Mountain? You can see it from our place at Tula. I've heard about the spirits there, and how they will protect the people.

"I wonder what Yveth has seen..."

"Dad! Your Policía phone is vibrating! Should I answer it?" Dyna, Nito's 12 year old daughter, called.

"I'll get it. Thanks. I should have it on ring."

Nito went into the sala and answered the special cell phone with the police departments at Buabidi and Soloy. It would be something some tourist did. There were a lot of tourists in Buabidi because of the museum [*Dead Man Talking - Clint Faraday Mysteries book 51*]. That was, by far, the place where most violent crime took place.

"Oye. Tica Nito."

"Nito, this is Moises, in Buabidi. I am calling because there is a strange murder of a person from here and a man from Suiza. It was at Misty Mountain, near Quebrada Tula.

"I have little information, but it seems to have some kind of connection with the stories about the spirits there.

"It is confused. Luana says she will not go there, because the sprits are angered, and her power is painful when she thinks about it.

"I will send the helicopter for you, if you will go there?"

Nito's father had often used the government/police helicopters. He was a multimillionaire, and more often paid for their use. Nito would pay for this, because he would go to his own home there. He agreed, and said he would be ready in an hour, and it would take most of that for the chopper to arrive, anyhow.

"The Panameño body is Juan Carlos Gutieriz, from Santiago. He was a sort of guide for special tours into other places in Panamá. As you know, those places do not include the comarca, except a few places like there at Cusapín that tourists like," Moises explained. They were at the morgue in Soloy. "He was killed, as you can see, with a machete.

"The tourist is a Suiza called Sven Harstedt. We have no cause of death. He was in the same room as Gutieriz, in a house that was unused at this time of year. It is in a small puebla called Pajaro Verde. The village is mostly deserted at this time.

"We know nothing more, except Harstedt has been in Panamá for three months. He was in Panamá City for one week, then in Bocas for three weeks, then in David until he went to Soloy four days ago. He then is found dead in Pajaro Verde."

"I see," Nito replied. "I'll go to David first. That's probably where he found his reason to go to Pajaro.

"Do you know about any of his contacts in David? Where he stayed?"

"No, but you can do a passport search for where he stayed, if it was a hotel."

"What was in his effects? Can I get access quickly?"

"Yes. I have it here. I knew you would want to see it."

They went to the property room, where Moises took the evidence box from a locker and handed it to Nito, who was beginning to get an exasperated look on his face.

Moises laughed. "We did a complete CSI before we moved anything. Definitely before we put it in the box. You have taught us that much!

"There were no fingerprints or DNA sources not accounted for."

Nito nodded. The box had the passport, a wallet, two sets of keys, a handkerchief, a wristwatch, two cell phones, a small penknife, and some coins. There was a list of the contents of the wallet, along with smaller lists of where each item led, the numbers from the cell phones, both sent and received. There were two hundred six dollars in the wallet as dollars, and forty Rias, plus a

20,000 peso note from Colombia.

"Well, the motive wasn't robbery," Nito said. "The look of the body tells us it wasn't a rage killing. It was neat and fast. These are pictures of the Panamanian victim when he was brought in? No rage there, either.

"Where else has he been, using that passport? – Here it is. Listed. Here, Colombia, Mexico, The states, England, Germany, and Switzerland. Italy for one day.

"Did you find where his luggage is stored?"

"Yes. That note at the bottom. Hotel Buena Vista, in Soloy. Not anything that told us much. Ordinary types of clothes for a tourist from that area. Two thousand dollars in cash. Some semi-expensive jewelry. Some tourist items, like bead bracelets. Two chargers for the cell phones. A notebook. Toshiba. Three years old. We printed out the history. He mostly did e-mail and visited Twitter and LinkedIn, but didn't seem to use them, only to lurk. He made travel plans through computer booking ... I see we didn't connect something that I'm equally sure you will have noted. He booked to Brasil for two days, which will explain the Rias."

"And that he had another passport."

Moises looked a little shocked, then nodded. "I think perhaps ... there is far more to this picture than a flower in the rain."

"*What the..*! Where did you get that one?!"

"I heard it somewhere. I've always wanted a situation where I could use it!"

Nito gave him the bird. They both laughed. "We have to find that other passport. I don't ... yes! I do! Let's fire up the notebook!"

Moises looked a question at him, then said, "We have to go to the station. The notebook is there.

"Might I ask what you've discovered?"

"He booked through the comp. I want to see the booking to Brasil. It will contain the number of...."

"... *The passport* he was using!"

"Bingo. Let's go! I also want to know which sites he visited."

They headed for the station. Nito got the computer notebook and checked the passport used for Brasil. Hans Goberlenk, Germany.

The notebook had a divided memory/program section. Nito checked to open one. Not much to see that he could say had anything to do with the case. He called a good friend, an old computer genius who worked with his father, and asked how to get into the private section. He put the notebook online and waited while Doug ran a cookie search and decode.

"Write in oh-oh-four-handyman. When the

authorization box comes on, type in One-GermanTwo [he spelled out the necessary form] and you're in."

"Thanks, Doug. You just saved me hours."

He typed in and got access, then studied the history. It seemed confused. E-Bay and a few other such sites accounted for much of it. And PornHub and XNXX. There were several downloaded porn videos. It seemed as though "Hans" liked spanking vids. Moises came in just as he loaded one, and grinned at him.

"Might as well watch something interesting while I wait," he said. Moises gave him the finger.

He studied the things Harstedt was using the search for. They were general until just about six months before, when he concentrated on several items. One, in particular, caught Nito's eye.

"Moises, I want a close look at those trinkets!"

"You found something?"

"I might have."

"What?"

"I wish I knew!"

"I see. They're real stones, not the regular plastic beads," Moises said. "Why don't they refract ... your father had a case where real jewels were sprayed with clear acrylic paint so they would think they were fakes."

"Yes. That's real jade and amethysts, which aren't uncommon. I don't think I see what this would do, so far as smuggling jewels or such. There has to be more to it than that. Nobody is going to kill anyone over a few semi-precious stones, though Dad had the case with that amethyst [*Where Death Waits* book 50 Clint Faraday Mysteries] that was worth millions. That was close to Buabidi, not here.

"There is a story, very old, I'm told, of a strange jewel lost on Misty Mountain, and that the finder of the jewel will find a treasure beyond value that can never be collected and used.

"That doesn't make sense, but the story suggests the treasure is a lesson to the greedy from the ancient spirits, or something.

"I wonder if ... the beads are real jewels. Amethyst is found near Buabidi, and is supposed to be the favorite of spirits there. Is there ... then why ... We'll have to see."

"Then we are missing something."

"Yes. I have an little idea ... he bought the beads from ... littlecutethingsinternational dot com. I don't ... they seem a bit heavy, but it's hard to tell ... maybe ... it's not silver. I want to know what those little separators are made ... Moises, let me see that tie-tac!"

"It's real silver and turquoise. It *is* a little heavy. Real white gold? It's shiny enough, and silver tarnishes. Would that be motive enough?"

"Depends on the size of the lode."

He got the tie-tac and studied it. He scratched it with his penknife.

"It's harder than gold. I don't think Panamá has platinum. Does it? I've never heard of it here."

"There's a little, but it's near Volcan Baru."

"Maybe Baru *and...*?"

Moises looked surprised, then nodded slowly. "Platinum is a treasure beyond value – that could never be used by the ancient people, because they could not refine it. Now *I* begin to wonder!"

"I think I have enough to go to David, now. I know a place or two to look.

"There's about half an ounce of platinum in this thing, and platinum's more than two thousand an ounce or more. Even a small lode would be damned valuable."

David

Nito booked into the Pension Costa Rica, for old time's sake. His father had stayed there often, and he had sometimes been with him. Lee's son, Brett, was running the place now. David was just too much a city. Nito, like his father and mother, didn't like cities.

"Hi, Nito! Long time, no see!" Brett greeted. "Got some murders in David they asked you to look into?

"Your sister was here a couple of weeks ago. She looks a lot like your Mom. They called her to help with the design of the new hospital. It'll have a wing that treats holistically and with plants. Dave's cancer cure, you know."

"Yes. Nicole told me about it. We talked about Dave, but mostly about the orchids and music. Fifteen years, and the drug companies are still fighting to have the cure outlawed. It's knocked them out of the chemotherapy business here.

"Brett, do you remember a Swiss by the name of Harstedt who stayed here about a month ago?"

"That big blonde guy who tried too hard to be liked?"

"I know he was big and blonde. I need to know more about him. Who he saw. Where he went."

"'Was'? He murdered?"

"Uh-huh."

"I didn't really pay much attention to him. I think he went to the Park Vista a lot. His Spanish was pretty bad. He said he collected bead jewelry, and wanted to see Dad's collection. He only had two or three bracelets. He looked at Dad's stuff, and you could tell he didn't have a clue about beads.

"He wanted to see the ones made into things, but Dad just collected the beads. I sort of forgot about him. He was just someone who wanted to impress people. I remember that he could have a lot of friends if he would just loosen up and be himself.

"He was friends with that Jon character for awhile, I think. It doesn't take long for people to see through that one.

"He met with an Indio with a Jewish name."

"Jewish name? A lot of us have Jewish and English names, in a way. Smith and Bosman, Trotman, Taylor."

"It wasn't really Jewish. It sounded like Jewish. Guttermann? Gudman?"

"Gutieriz?"

"That could be. Why?"

"Gutieriz was murdered at the same time.

Anyone else?"

Brett looked thoughtful, then said he once saw him talking with a bigshot local con man. Jesus Cruiz.

"Fat pig who hangs around the Manicucci bunch of wannabe mafia?"

"Uh-huh. Five minutes, you like him, and are a good buddy. Ten and things seem a bit out of focus. He can't quite keep his story straight. Knows every crook in Panamá from Noriega to Martinelli. Close personal friends. Learned a lot from Noriega, personally."

"And he would have to have been three years old when Noriega taught him all that stuff. Know the type. Much too well, in the cop business. Thanks."

He headed for the Park Vista. Beads had been pretty much ... no! Only those that were used in bracelets or whatever!

He cancelled the Park Vista. Cruiz wouldn't be there. He would be out toward the stadium – and it would be too early for him, now. Or he would be around the casinos, which meant he would be dining at La Tipica for lunch, and one of the higher class restaurants for dinner.

He called Moises to ask if Harstedt had a Panamanian bank account.

"No, but Goberlenk did. Let me find it. I'll call

back in about half an hour."

"Thanks. I'll get some coffee and hojaldras.

"Nito? Banco Global. I'll text the number and a scan of his death certificate under the Policía Nacionál logo. I suppose the department has looked into it, but there's no note about it. I'll get Judge Gomez to issue a court order identification. You are now acting in your capacity as a police investigator, officially. I owe you a dollar."

That was cool [did anyone say that anymore?] – and he *was* a police officer, just in another department.

He went to an internet café and received the text and download. He had the court order and his official recognition papers printed out. The Global Bank was just four blocks away, so he got there fast.

There was the usual delay/obstruction rigamarole, but he soon got a printout of the activity in the account for the past two years, then headed for the pension.

It seems that Goberlenk/Harstedt had an account that had more than six hundred thousand dollars USA in it two years ago. It varied up or down no more than $50K until five months ago, when there was a drop of $150K, followed in two weeks by a deposit of four million dollars. It stayed at four-five until three weeks ago, then dropped to $25K.

What happened to that money?

He went through the account carefully. The only hint was a code number for four million five hundred thousand dollars.

Here we go! Bureaucrap!

He went back to the bank, where he discussed code numbers. It turned out, after four hours, to have been a cash transfer.

Why not tell him that from the first? Why would they try to hide ...?

Ah! Who *received* that transfer?

He wasn't about to go the bank again. It was closed at four for all business.

Doug! Could he hack the account? Nito knew he did for his father, a couple of times.

He called him. "Doug, can you find what happened to a cash transfer of four and a half mil they are trying to keep from me?"

"Give me a number, and you never called me today! That's ridiculous!"

"Code for the transfer?"

"Perfect. Take all of thirty seconds."

Nito read him the code. "Global Bank."

"Yes. That is the first letter and three numbers. To Bank of Colombia. Investors Unified Creators, SA, and Frederico Garcia Fine Accessories, SA.

"There's a legal note that twenty grand went to

the account of Milcare Suarez, Panamá City, for commission."

"And there's the one they're trying to hide. I would thank you, but there would be no point, seeing you never answered the phone."

Doug laughed and rang off.

So! Who the hell was Milcare Suarez?

He would have to use some kind of disguise. His picture had been on TV and in the papers too much for him to think they wouldn't know who Clinton Faraday was. He had never used one before, but his father had. He knew how to look a lot different than he looked now. His voice was ordinary, so change it to one just very slightly different. Remember not to do the unconscious mannerisms that were part of his personality. Add a couple of things, and remember to always act in the manner of that character. He could make himself look more out of shape, and maybe heavier. With that, he would also look shorter. He always wore a minimum for the place, so would wear a suit. He never wore jewelry, so would wear some, but not too much. He could change his walk like CD Grimes taught him when he was a kid.

Then he would meet a certain person. He would be the type with a bit of money who thought he knew everything and was smarter than anyone else in this third world hole.

Where was he headed? Not Boquete. The type would think they were all schnooks who didn't know their ass from a cowflop when it came to business. Bocas? That was a bit farther ... which made it perfect! That would be a place where some egocentric wealthy nutcase might go, looking to invest where the money would be found [not understanding that backpackers and surfers didn't have all that money to spend, which was why so many of the type went home in six months, broke, and with their tail between their legs. Half the hotels on Isla Colón were for sale, cheap, because the demographics weren't checked]. He would, of course, know better than to invest *that* way, because he *did* study the demographics.

So! He would be a schnook with a lot of money he inherited who was going to become *the* business tycoon here! After all, he saw how his uncle, who left him all that money, built a business with a little investment and clever manipulation [maybe not always so aboveboard and honest] to a very profitable level.

So! On to Bocas!

The somewhat flabby, dark man flicked an invisible ash off his perfectly tailored suit shoulder as he walked up the ramp into the Toro Loco Bar and Restaurant with a superior sneer on his face. The Cuban cigar held between the perfectly manicured fingers with the large ruby and onyx ring blatantly displayed made quite a statement.

"You can't come inside the bar with that cigar lit," Nilsa informed him. He shrugged and tossed the $12.50 cigar into the street.

"I would like Corona Gold Special and something to eat. The fare on that plane was, shall we say, less than adequate."

Nilsa handed him a menu. She got a Corona beer from the cooler, and he said, "No! Corona *Gold Special*! I can't drink that common horse urine!"

"Then go to Mexico. That's the only place to get the Gold Special," Charlie, a regular Nito knew, said in a bit of a threatening tone.

Nito looked shocked and scandalized. "I suppose the common people here wouldn't know ... oh, well. What would you suggest?"

"That you go someplace else, but you might like Amstel Light. It has that slightly acid flavor."

"Er, yes. Thank you.

"Is the cameranos al ahiolieo good here? Garlic shrimp. I just can't get the Spanish right!"

"If you like that kind of thing, it's very good," Alice Bowens, another regular, said drily. "Are you a gringo – or British?"

"Actually, I'm Canadian, but was raised in the United States, New Hampshire, and England. Stropshire. I just inherited a little money when my Uncle Ralph died. Only a couple of million pounds, but that should be enough for an investment, and a friend who was here for awhile said this was the place to invest."

"Oh. Going to build a hotel?" Charlie asked, with a sneer.

"*Here*!? Where half of them go broke the first six months? Wrong demographics. Backpackers and surf bums don't spend fifty dollars a night in a hotel. I *do* know business!"

"Got a plan, or just looking?" Alice asked. "Marinas go broke pretty fast, too."

"Just looking for ideas. Natural resources or land. Something that will grow over time."

"There's some gold and a lot of silver toward Puerto Armuelles. There's some zinc. Food retail is pretty well tied up by the Chinese. Wholesale could do something. They raise a lot of teak on the Pacific side. Don't fall for the scam on the Caribbean side," a dark smooth type said easily. "Teak's no good here."

"Yes. Too wet, and teak needs a hard dry season. I've looked at that. There's a place called Hornitos where they raise a lot of teak. They tried pine up there, but it has to be treated or the termites will eat it away in a week. I'm James Harold Matthews."

"Felix Dumas. Means happy, but I'm not too much of the time. Had some famous ancestors, but I'm just a regular kind of person."

They started chatting. Charlie and Alice wandered away. Charlie pointed to Dumas and wagged a finger when his back was turned. Nito raised an eyebrow, and they went to sit at a table.

This was obviously one of the scam artists in the area. Nito had to act like he was suspicious, but possibly interested. Dumas wasn't who he wanted to meet, but might lead him to the one he *did* want to meet. A guy named Milcare Suarez, who was supposed to be on Isla Colón, at the time.

"Well, James, I dabble a bit in some investment things. Lot of people won't trust anyone but me among the gringos. You wouldn't believe the scams!" Dumas said. "There are people here who bought property twenty years ago and end up in court every year because of some claim by an Indio that his great grandfather grew a banana tree there once, so it's his. Always win, but after a couple thousand dollars in court and lawyer costs."

"I'm aware of that. I read *Fading Paradise* years ago, and got the latest update. The man who wrote it died about the time I read the last update.

"I wouldn't invest in land in Bocas del Toro, and probably not in Chiriqui, unless it's titled, and even that can be a little shaky. I'm interested in business or minerals or whatever. Timber is pretty well tied up, but maybe something for export made from local woods. My uncle had some things made in Honduras – mahogany, you know – shipped in. Made out fairly well."

"Well, I can probably find something. I've heard some rumors. Not too strictly, shall we say, according to Hoyle with the government, but one hell of a potential.

"I'll be honest with you. I'll get a finder's fee. A good one!"

"And get a commission from whoever, too. I know business. If it has the potential, and isn't too risky in other ways, that's part of the deal."

"I'll check out the word and get back to you. Do you have a cell phone?"

"Yes. Of course. I have a cheap one. I don't do

business on the net, because anyone can hack into that in minutes. I'm also damned careful what I say on the phone. I don't leave the chip in when I go places I don't care for the world to know about." [That would be in character for both! "I" seven times in one paragraph!]

"I don't see ...?"

"Every time you use the thing, the GPS location registers on the relay satellite. That's why you can be found anywhere, within a few feet. The chip responds. Take it out, and you're off the system. Carry a couple you buy from the street venders. Use them instead."

"I never thought of that! I knew to never say anything or type anything you didn't want seen or heard, because there are ten government agencies listening to all of it."

"Yes. I'll be in touch later. What's your cell number?"

Dumas gave him the number. He took out a fifteen dollar cheap cellular and did a "one ring" that registered on Dumas' phone, a three hundred dollar modern type with a big screen, so he marked it and looked sheepish.

They went their own ways. Nito was still looking for Milcare Suarez. Dumas was the same type, so might lead him to a meeting.

Nito saw several people he knew well, and managed to not be recognized. He knew how to irritate most of them by being the type of arrogant asshole he was disguised as.

The second day later, Dumas called him and asked if he was still interested in an investment that could be a bigger fortune than anything he ever considered before. No hint of what on the phone, as he knew. It was a property in a perfect location is all he would say.

He'd told Dumas he wouldn't invest in land, so that was for the phone. Dumas was easy to manipulate. The type always were. They would meet in an hour in the cemetery. [Which showed how much of the surveillance talk had registered with Dumas. If there was anyone listening, they would know to have someone at the cemetery in an hour, so not saying it on the phone was wasted.]

So! How to dress like a naive egocentric millionaire with no better taste than a catfish?

He put on loud Bermuda shorts and a louder floppy shirt that featured hibiscus flowers. He could claim he got the outfit in Hawaii.

Nito soon headed for the cemetery. He would see who "happened" to be there. He knew he wasn't specially tagged, but was Dumas?

Dumas was close to the morgue, wearing a

floppy hat and sunglasses. He was trying to look like a local farmer, so as to not be noticed.

Nito always noticed. Nobody else there yet, so maybe Dumas wanted to see if anyone showed up. Ten minutes to the hour, Nito walked back to the road to the airport and got a taxi.

At four minutes to the hour, Nito got out of the taxi in front of the cemetery. Dumas was just inside, dressed as usual, with a thin slick type. They could be brothers, but that was just the type. They didn't share many features.

And this was a great stroke of luck! He couldn't be sure, but this one looked like the only fuzzy picture he'd seen of Suarez!

Nito had peripheral vision not much less than his father. He noticed the expression on Suarez' face as he was paying the taxi. He turned and looked directly at Dumas, then strolled by them like he didn't see them. Dumas would think that was because he hadn't said anyone else would be there. Nito was being cautious.

"Mr. Matthews!" Dumas called. "I talked to you in the Toro Loco Tuesday night!" He raised an eyebrow in question.

Nito smiled and said, "Yes! You're that artist – no. Same name as a writer. Dumas.

"It's a beautiful day. I decided to come here to see if there were any famous people buried here.

Didn't stop to think that I wouldn't know who they were if I was staring at their crypt!

"I can be dense sometimes."

"This is a friend, Milcare Suarez. He knows a little about investments. He has something you might find interesting." He raised the eyebrow again.

"I didn't know who you were with. Might have been somebody who just was here, or might have been someone who wanted to know things we don't want them to know. Got to be careful, or you miss the ground floor."

That seemed to satisfy both Dumas and Suarez.

"Let's go back near the bay. We can have some privacy there," Suarez suggested. "I want to show you something."

They strolled to the back and sat on a crypt for Suarez to hand Nito a tie clip just like the one found on Harstedt. He hid his glee and managed to take it and just shrug.

"That was made with things found in a certain isolated area that had never been explored for minerals," Suarez said. "Do you know what it is?"

"Hmm. Turquoise. That's not a very stable investment."

"No. We have a ton of the stuff. Note the weight of the thing."

"Hmm. White gold? That could be big in today's

market."

"It's a lot harder than gold, and a little heavier. It's also worth double what gold is bringing."

"Really? Platinum? I heard there was some here, but very small deposits. Volcan Baru. Not here."

"What has been found and mined was Volcan Baru." Dumas said. "Before."

"It would have to be ... not even a very large deposit. Crude ore is always nearly pure and would bring about eighteen hundred. There's no way you can process it. That's only done in a couple of places."

"We could process it with the newer laser technology, but there's enough that we aren't really interested in processing it. Englehart does that, in Colombia. We have a way to get it to Colombia. They check things coming in from there very close, and almost ignore things going there from here."

"Why would you even give a hot damn about an investor?"

"We have no funds. It's that simple. It's like the Indio you talked to in the park this morning. [He looked a little nervous at that slip, but Nito knew he was being watched.] He has about four million dollars worth of property, and has to count his change if he wants a beer.

"Once we get it set up, it'll keep on by itself. It's

a matter of getting it set up. We have a few pieces like what you are holding. We could sell them for the funds, but that would alert the wrong people to the fact we have it."

Nito nodded. That was true – but why kill anyone? They apparently got the funding.

"What do you think it will take? I have a little put aside, but it's not unlimited."

"About two million dollars – so you see our problem. I doubt you would have that much, but we can get a couple of others in as partners, and can do it with some from each.

"That cuts down on the individual percentage, but you do what you have to do."

"Oh, I have that. We would be better off, as you said, keeping as many out as we can."

"We have the product, you have the funding. We aren't greedy. You get fifty percent, and we split the other fifty. Does that sound reasonable?"

"Fifty one. I will want a certain amount of control, and you can't vote me out, that way."

"Well, I think we can do that!"

"So! Let's go have a beer! I look like an idiot with this crap I wore in Hawaii – and don't give a damn!

"You do understand this is all contingent of a little investigation on my part?"

"We wouldn't do business with you, at all, if it

weren't, " Suarez answered. "Someone who has no knowledge of business would go into a deal without investigation, and that would mean it would be screwed up so bad everyone would lose their ass!"

They slapped palms with that, and headed for The Pirate for a couple beers.

They would meet in David in three days. They could make a plan on how to approach this. They could make arrangements for Nito to go to the site to see for himself that this was no scam!

"I'll say, right here, that the lode is on the Indio property. Comarca. I have an agreement that I can take anything, so far as minerals go, that I can carry, personally. That doesn't mean I can take a truck in and haul out a load or two. It's also in a place where you couldn't get a truck to, anyhow," Suarez said. "If we three go in, and each carry out just fifty pounds ... well!"

"Hmmm. Three and a half mil per trip, more or less. Are we limited to how many trips we can make?"

Nito knew that kind of arrangement could be made, but very sincerely doubted such as Suarez had any such agreement. He also knew that, except in rare cases, it was a one-trip deal.

"There are three of us. We can make three trips, minimum," Dumas said. "I think there's no limit, really, but the Indios will be suspicious, and can cut it off.

"Hell! If we make three trips we get a ten million return on your two, which leaves us with eight mil, of which you get four. I think my two mil will take pretty good care of me for life! I would live four times better than now on just the interest!"

"This should leave me with a little more, so I'd probably buy some property and build my dream house. I like Panamá! I could live very well down here, and the women, particularly the Indio-Latina mix, are fantastic!

"Oh, yeah! I could get into that!" Nito said. "Hey! Girl! Another round here – and put a little rum in this one!"

"I'll want to see what is there, personally. I'll put the two mil in a special account, and will simply add your name to the account when I approve it, if that's okay. Transfer funds within my own company, so no taxes or government snooping. I've learned how to get around a lot of that kind of thing," Nito explained. "You say we can go to the place tomorrow?"

"Yes. We go to David tonight, then get an early bus to the comarca. Soloy, then a minibus to Quebrada Tula. We can take horses from there to the lode."

"Why not rent a car? Wouldn't that ... I see! Don't look too anxious, and don't give away that this is anything but a vacation tour or something. Nobody will pay us any attention!" Nito agreed.

"They'll pay attention on the comarca. We *aren't* Indios, but you could pass as one. Do you have Indio blood?" Dumas asked. "You can act like a tourist on an adventure. Misty Mountain is impressive, and it has a couple of picturesque waterfalls and a stone grotto kind of thing in the river that makes the international attraction at

Gualaca seem insignificant. Several caves. That kind of thing."

"There's an international attraction at Gualaca?" Nito asked. "I know there's teak there...?

"I have some AmerInd blood. Hopi, I'm told. Great grandfather."

"The Changeleones," Dumas said.

"Oh! I think I saw something about that on TV. At the airport, when I got here."

"Well, we get the four o'clock bus at Almirante. We'll be in David about seven thirty. I've got the tickets for the bus, and we're booked into the Iris Hotel for tonight," Dumas said. "We catch the Soloy bus at six thirty in the morning, and stay in Soloy tomorrow night, then take the bus to Quebrada Tula. We can rent horses there, and should be at the mountain by five or so in the afternoon. We camp in a little shack there for the night, go to the lode, and can take a little out with us, but not enough to notice. No more than a pound apiece.

"We can make the next trip in two more days. I'll explain to Edmondo – he's the local chief – that we found some stuff we want to have analyzed, because it might be valuable. He'll okay it."

"Why not cut him into it? We can make more trips, that way," Nito suggested.

"He isn't interested. They don't use money there, and that would be the only thing to use that I can think of. He knows there's platinum there, but says it isn't good for anything, because they can't melt it, so they can't make anything with it. He says it turns black if you get it hot, and it's not a pretty black."

"Yeah. platinum turns black when you get it too hot in air," Nito said. "Should I take my pistol along?"

"Christ, no!" Dumas cried. "If they catch you with a gun on the comarca they might just execute you without a trial or anything! You can't get away with the same things here as on the comarca!"

"They can...? Oh. I heard that the laws here don't apply on the comarca. You mean it's true?"

"Yes. A lot of it."

"Well, four o'clock in Almirante. We get the three o'clock water taxi?"

"Yes," Suarez replied. "Don't take along a lot of stuff. We can leave anything we won't need in David, when we go to the comarca. There's a baggage check at the terminal."

"I'll go clean up and pack. I'll meet you at the water taxi at a quarter to three.

"Which one?"

"Taxi twenty five. Near the police station,"

Dumas said.

"I came here on it. Okay!"

Nito talked with two friends from Isla Colón at the bus terminal in Almirante. He told them the reason he was in disguise was to catch a murderer, and it seems there are at least two. Don't give him away.

The Indios use slightly different features in identification, so his disguise didn't work with them, though they knew there was a reason for it, and that Latinos or gringos wouldn't know it was a disguise. Obilio and Stefan had worked with Clint's father, at times, and had good connections, even among the Indios, who were very connected, in many ways.

Dumas and Suarez had gone into Almirante to see and "old friend" before catching the bus. Nito asked Obilio if he knew who they saw there.

"Sometimes, that Robinson ladron. There's some fat pig they call 'Jesus' there now. Thinks he's a mafia chief, or something. As your father said, tyranosaurus mouth and gecko ass!"

Uh-oh! Jesus Cruiz? Was he getting himself into a spot he couldn't get out of?

"Thanks. I needed to know that. He might be behind a couple of murders, and I can see where such as Suarez and Dumas get their funding.

"Bilio, I can't use my phone. they might have it listened to. Can you call Edmondo, at Tula, and have us watched when we get there? Don't let them know they're being watched."

"Sure, Nito. We can watch them, starting now. I think Solbiero will be on the bus to David, and we'll have somebody there."

"I might have bitten off more than I can chew. I'm good at police work, procedural, but this PI stuff is a different cow in a different pasture."

"Take great care, my friend. We will always be here if you need us, as we know you will always be there for us."

"There is Donaldo Robinson. In the taxi. He may be watching you," Stefan hissed, as a taxi came to beside where they were talking. He pointed to the store across the road and said, a little loudly, "They sell them there. Any store," and he and Obilio walked away as Robinson got out of the cab. Nito shook his head, and went to the store, bought a disposable razor, and returned to the terminal as Dumas and Suarez got out of a cab. He waved and went to them.

The bus came in three more minutes, and they got on.

Nothing in Chiriqui Grande. Nito moved from his seat next to a fat woman with a baby when people got off the bus there.

At the terminal at David, they got together and headed for the Hotel Iris. TJ, at the Park Vista Bar, had smoked chicken on the menu. Delicious. They all had it and were having a beer when Cruiz came in. Dumas acted surprised to see him, and invited him to their table to introduce him.

Nito felt a little evil. "I see you got here as fast as we did! You didn't take the bus...? Oh. Private car?"

"Er ... I don't...?"

"I saw you in Almirante yesterday when I was going to the water taxi. You're distinctive enough that I could hardly miss you!

"You were going into that fish supply place, or the shop next to it."

"Oh, yes! I get fresh seafood right off the boat. Really good!" He raised an eyebrow at Dumas, who looked exceedingly nervous, all of a sudden. "I don't really notice people when I go anywhere.

"Are you staying in David long?"

"Oh, come and go. I might stay here, or I might go looking at the sites. I heard there were a lot of gringos in Boquete. Met a couple, in fact. If they're all like them, I don't think I care to see the place."

They chatted a bit. Nito "innocently" kept them wondering what the hell he was doing. Finally, Suarez said, "Er, James – Sr. Cruiz is someone we may need. He is the person who can move the, er, the silver out for us."

"Oh. Sorry! I was just deliberately confusing you, in case you were just trying to, you know."

"You're *very* good at *that*!" Cruiz laughed. "I was wondering if you had a drug problem or were drunk!

"You are with two dreamers, you know. Always looking for the big strike! Gonna become billionaires next week, when they find the El Dorado lode!

"They have brought in a little silver, and a little gold, but they're getting it from the comarca, and they can only bring what they can carry, which means maybe a thousand dollars or so, There are a lot of little lodes on the comarca.

"It will be a fun adventure, probably, but you won't be getting anything close to a million dollar lode!"

Dumas looked smug, Suarez grinned at Nito.

"*Oh*! Well ... I thought I could get a couple billion real fast, and spend the rest of my life running around on yachts or my private jet and such! Damn!"

They all laughed.

After an hour of that, Nito went to the hotel. They would meet at the terminal at a quarter after six in the morning. Soloy bus.

At the terminal, Enrique, a close friend from near Quebrada Tula, saw him come in with Dumas and Suarez. He made a "passing glance" in Nito's direction, then started talking with the other Indios waiting for the bus. Nito and friends were ignored.

They got on the bus, and Nito's seat was next to Enrique. Dumas and Suarez were together three rows back. Nito acted like he wanted to talk with Enrique, who was a little cold toward him, but they did chat a bit just before they reached Soloy. They exchanged a lot of information in very low voices that wasn't seen or heard a row back, much less three.

The minibus to Quebrada Tula is every second hour, so they were at the stop for more than an hour, then were headed for Tula. This time, they were together, but with a very tight crowd. Nito had fun, but Dumas and Suarez very obviously did *not*! Jahira was on one side of him, and Suarez the other, in the back seat. Jahira recognized him, but was warned that he was in disguise for a reason, so she acted like a very curious girl who wanted to flirt with the extrañero. They laughed a lot, Nito pretending he couldn't understand her, and she talking a lot in dialect [which Nito was very fluent in] when she wanted to say anything real.

In Tula, Dumas got three horses for them to use from Edmondo, who ignored Nito's existence almost to the point of rudeness. Edmondo had to go to the city fairly often as chief, so could use the money.

They set out as soon as they could, and made it through the fantastic scenery to Misty Mountain just before dark. There was a small shed/hut there. They fixed some canned food and turned in for the night. It was uncomfortably tight, even though Nito was used to sleeping with others. These repulsed him.

After sopa china, in the morning, they set out around the mountain for about a kilometer to a narrow cave by a stream.

"There it is!" Suarez announced.

They dismounted, tied the horses, and went into the cave. It was a lot of rubble and loose rock for about ten meters, then opened up slightly. The lanterns showed a lot of white quartz, with a few seams of greyish metal. It looked more like zinc than platinum, but Nito had never seen platinum in its natural form.

He took out his pocket knife and scratched the metal.

"Zinc? This isn't platinum!"

"No. The platinum's farther back. Actually, this is zinc that's contaminated with rhodium," Dumas said. "We wanted to see if you knew the difference."

They went another thirty five meters, and were standing in what looked like an ancient stream bed. The bottom had small pockets filled with greyish gravel.

"Pick up a handful of the pebbles," Suarez suggested.

It was heavy. *Very* heavy.

"Ninety seven point four percent pure," Dumas said. "There's about twelve times this area with the pockets. You can see that this one has at least fifteen pounds of the stuff.

"I suggest you look over the rest, then we each take a couple of ounces and head back for David. Don't take enough that it will be seen that you have the weight. I'd suggest we each take a half pound or less. Distribute it in your pockets – but remember, it is *heavy*, and will tear the pocket.

"You can have an assay in David. That will prove this is no scam – and you will have ten thousand dollars worth of it.

"Let's not even discuss anymore here. We can come back in a couple of days and take out our first load."

They agreed. Nito looked over the rest of the area, picked up about half a pound, and they headed back to David.

Nito had noticed something farther back in the cave, and had managed to pick up a few nuggets back there when he dropped his flashlight.

He was damned glad he didn't have the money where they could get it. He saw what they were doing.

Were Gutieriz and Harstedt the first? It seemed a little too familiar a routine for that to be true.

"Well! I guess this will prove that your fat friend was wrong!" Nito cried. "There really *is* a huge fortune here for the taking!"

<u>*Explanations Needed*</u>

"Well, that was a very fast assay!" Nito declared next mid-day. They were at the testing laboratory, where he had given the woman in charge one of the pieces of gravel he had picked up at Misty Mountain.

"Yes. Ninety seven point five. A little better than my figure!" Dumas said, and giggled. "We can take this chart to my contact from Colombia, then we can get a deal with Sr. Cruiz."

"What kind of deal can we make with him?" Nito asked.

"Oh, I think we can make it a percentage deal. Maybe two percent?"

"From my part, of course?"

"No. That wouldn't be fair. One from us, and one from you."

Leaving me with a one percent deficit when he votes with you on anything. Uh-huh.

"We'll work that out for the contract," Dumas said, offhandedly. "Shall we go to a good restaurant, have a good meal, and work out the details? We'll want to get started as soon as possible."

"Yes. I think that would be best. We can agree on things, then contract Sr. Cruiz, finalize it, and go after our first load!" Suarez said. "I want to get this done as soon as we can. I'll be needing some funds soon. The place I want to buy has some gringos looking at it, and they'll pay a lot more than I could. If I get a deposit on it, it's mine!"

"Lead on!" Nito replied heartily. "We can answer all the questions, then get this boat in the water! I feel *good* about this!"

They decided to eat at La Tipica. The food was good, and they could have some privacy, while sitting at a table that was open to view publicly. It was late enough that they could get a table away from others.

When they were seated and the food was on the way, Suarez took out a standard blank contract form. He agreed to the wording as to who did what, until they came to the percents. He got stubborn about it, ending them up with a deadlock.

"There's enough here that we won't have a problem!" Suarez suggested. "You just supply a half percent, leaving you with forty nine five, and we and we take the one and a half, leaving us, combined, with forty eight five, so you still out-vote us."

Nito looked suspicious, but said that would be

alright, he supposed.

Then came the "Deposit" of 2 million dollars.

He looked thoughtful, and said, "We could have carried more than that out when we were there, and still be within the agreement of what we could take. I know there will be plenty of other expenses, but two million is a bit excessive – unless there's something I don't know?"

"Er, that is, we have to have the money to guarantee Sr. Cruiz will get paid if anything goes wrong. A million and a half. We also have to have enough to where a sudden influx won't be noticed in the account. The guarantee money for Sr. Cruiz will stay there, but it will make the bank not ask questions if a few million more are added from what we can claim is funds from other branches of the company. That's a sort of standard procedure. The banks didn't have to investigate further than finding the funds we deposit are legitimate. If they're transfers from a major international company, there will *be* no challenges," Dumas said, smoothly. "We might give a nice gift to the person in authority at the bank for his help in expediting the process, if you get my drift. If we already have a couple million in the bank, that would be within the rules."

They made their agreement, each read it over very carefully, then they went to the notary to have it certified. Nito stalled just enough that, when they left the notary, there wasn't time to get to the bank, so that would have to be done in the morning.

Now, he had to get away enough to discuss things with his Indio friends, and with the police department head for violent crimes, and the head of the scam/fraud department.

He was thinking of a way to not seem suspicious when someone called, "Oye! Gringo! Que paso?"

It was a very pretty, sexy young India. Nando, a close friend, and one who was watching them [Nito had noticed him twice] was with her.

"Yes?" Nito answered. "Oh! You're that guy from the terminal when we went to Soloy!"

"Yes. This is a friend who asked that I introduce her to the handsome gringo. She is Nilsa. This is, uh, Frank, was it?"

"No. James. You can call me Jim. Pleased to meet such an attractive young lady!"

"Would you like to go to a dance bar I know about?" Nando asked. "Nilsa loves to dance. She would like to get to know you."

"I can't ... but we've finished business for today! Guys, I want to relax a bit. See you in the morning!"

Dumas called him over to say this was a prostitute and her pimp [which the Indios didn't have].

"I've been all over the world. I know what's going on! I think she'll be fun!"

Dumas grinned, and said, "Just so you know. Take care!"

Nito waved to Dumas and Suarez, and went off with Nando and Nilsa. They called a cab, and Nando was a bit distant, so Nito knew there was someone he hadn't spotted. Close.

When the taxi pulled off, Nando said there was a big black who seemed a little too interested in them. The one with the Bob Marley tee shirt and the orange Nike shoes. He might just be someone who was looking for an opportunity to mug him, or may be something else.

They made sure they weren't followed, went around a few blocks, and to the police station, where Nito very quickly made a report and projection of what would happen tomorrow. They then went to a little bar called Cielo's, where Nando called some friends. They made plans about tomorrow. He would *not* be allowed to leave if they went back to the lode.

"Why not?" Nando asked.

"Because there were possibly two little pockets with platinum, and a lot of pockets with something else. They reflected differently in the lantern light. I picked up a couple. They seemed to be lead with a greyish coating."

"What would they gain?" Nilsa asked.

"There's actually about a hundred thousand dollars worth of platinum there. I'll have two million in the bank in an account with their names on it.

"Nilsa, I'm doing this because they're suspected of murdering two people with this scheme. I hope to prove it. I would greatly prefer that I not be another victim while doing that."

"I reckon!" Nando said.

They stayed at Cielo's for another hour, then Nito was seen going into Maxitel with Nilsa. She left an hour and a half later, and Nito went to the Iris. It was just before three o'clock AM. The big black was lounging in the lobby. Nito didn't seem to notice him.

"Well! We can get to the bank, probably take an hour or so, then head for Misty Mountain!" Suarez greeted in the morning, just before 6:00AM. "Do you have anything to do before we go?

"I hope your night was pleasant? Not too expensive?"

"We went to a little bar called Cielo's, out past Universidad Latina," Nito replied. "Nilsa and I hit it off pretty well. Nando warmed up after he got to know me. We had a good time. It was a lot cheaper than I thought it would be.

"I want to buy a few things. The banks aren't open 'til eight, and most shops aren't, either. I think we can either stay in David one more night, or can stay in Soloy. The stuff's not going anywhere we don't take it, so one day is nothing."

"Er, I see. I suppose I'm a bit overanxious. We can leave for Soloy about four or so?"

"That should be okay. Meet at the terminal at a quarter to four?

"Oh! Yeah! Should I sell this stuff to ... I guess Cruiz doesn't buy it, directly. There's supposed to be a guy over by Ovaldia who buys raw precious metals. Him?"

"Sell it? I mean ... I think Sr. Cruiz will buy the small amounts we have, but why not just include it in the first shipment?"

"I'd have to take the money for what I want out of the account, and I'd rather not touch that unless I absolutely have to. Taking five or six grand is piddling, but it might make them watch the flow. I know how that works. Fifty thou, they consider normal. Five, they get suspicious.

"Bankers are weird. I know a lot of them in five or six countries, and they're all alike. They call it a 'window of doubt' between two and forty five mil. Andy Trevor, in London, is director of the banking international crap, and he showed me how there are what the call 'flags' that the computers react to.

"We had a sort of, I guess you'd call it, 'Gentleman's agreement' about some things. [He made it up as he went along.]

"See, I've arranged to link my company account, to merge it with this one. That will be a surprise to my partner, because she's been trying to screw me – in more than one way – out of the three million pounds that we, uh, sort of ... hid there.

"Taxes and all that, you see. She thinks she can get it all if something were to happen to me. She's been embezzling a bit, here and there. I'll leave a thousand pounds, in it and put all the rest in the account here. After all, we'll be adding ten million or so, so it's safest for me.

"I have that in transition, so don't have any cash until the account's opened, later today, then we have to wait another three days for it to be authenticated. I want a little to live on until then."

"Yes, uh, well, er ... I suppose I can ask Sr. Cruiz if he will, uh, advance what you need for what you have."

"Great! I have about four ounces. I figure, after commissions and fees and, like that, about five grand. Does that seem about right?"

"He'll probably okay that."

"He okays...?"

"*Uh*! Wrong term, ha, ha! He'll probably go for it! I think it's a good idea to keep it all in just our hands. Bringing in some little joyeria shop could make the wrong people want to know where it came from, heh, heh. [wink, wink]. With that other three million to be added – today, yet! – there can't be any serious objection to a couple thousand, for sure!

"I'll call him right now ... I have to call Dumas. He has Sr. Cruiz's number. Maybe he can call him. Just a minute."

He went to the side and made a call that included some arm waving, then came back to say that Sr. Cruiz would give Dumas the money. They could take the stuff from Nito to his room in about an hour and get the cash.

"I'll grab some breakfast and be back," Nito promised. "It that Amelia's Restaurante open this early?"

"I think, not until seven thirty. The only place I know that is open is the little typical restaurant on the corner behind Romero's. It'll depend on if you like the local food."

"Those jo-al-drums and coffee, maybe with some meatballs?"

"Yes. That's typical."

Nito waved and walked off.

He had put a little bump in their plans. They would *not* want any of the platinum sold. They needed it to seed the cave for the next sucker. They would have to give him five thousand, which was probably nothing to Cruiz, but interfered with his plans that would mean all money went in only his direction.

Rigoberto Carnales, an Indio friend from Soloy, came to sit next to him at the restaurant. He said, very quietly, that Nito was being followed by two people. A police woman and a big black. They were good, but not perfect.

Also: someone had contacted Beningno Flores, a part-Indio man who was suspected of many things, in Soloy. He was seen in David and Isla Colón with Cruiz, and once in David with Suarez. He had taken the early bus to Qubrada Tula. That was information from Jefe Mondo.

So. That was why Suarez seemed so concerned about the delay.

Berto touched Nito's knee with his and pointed to the door with a thumb. A woman was just coming in.

"The police woman?" Nito asked, and pointed to the sugar. Berto passed the sugar and nodded. They didn't look at each other. Berto touched Nito's knee again with his own, and laid the knife he was using to cut a meatball at an angle on his plate. It pointed out to the side where the taxis were dispatched. Nito casually looked around, and at the cab stand. He could just see a big black man's head, behind a taxi.

He finished his Hojaldres and bolitas, downed the last of the coffee, and called the girl over to pay his bill. He nodded curtly at Berto, and walked out. He stopped at the corner, after crossing the road, and watched as the police woman suddenly paid for her coffee and came out front.

He grinned at her. She grinned back. That would mean she was with the police, and was following him on directions from above. She wasn't trying to not be seen by him, she was trying to not be seen by anyone else who was paying too much attention to him.

He pointed toward the big black man with his thumb and went on toward the parque, stopping at the entrance to Romero's to talk with a woman selling lottery tickets. The police woman was by the door to the bar, Nito pointed to the black, just coming from the cab stand. She managed to step out in front of him and get bumped just enough to slip on the curb and fall to her knees. The black had little choice but to help her up. She was "apologizing profusely" and picking up things spilled from her purse. Nito went quickly to the parque, then around the corner toward the local bus stop. He managed to be getting on the Pedregal bus as the black came to the corner.

He rode the bus four blocks and got off when it stopped for a stop street where there were a number of people waiting to cross the street. He stepped behind the corner of the store there and waited until a taxi with the black inside went by.

He went back toward the parque. The police woman was in a taxi. She spotted him, and the cab stopped. He got in, and said, "Hotel Castilla."

He chatted with Vonny, and learned that she was to protect him from some very dangerous people, and to report everything any of them did.

"Cruiz?" Nito asked.

"Uh-huh. Him and that Pontes character from Colombia. They're as thick as the thieves they are."

Nito laughed. They talked a bit, and he got out to stroll around awhile, waiting for the bank to open.

He didn't care if he was followed, and if they knew everyone he met, really. What was it to them if he accidentally met with some random Indios at a restaurant?

He wanted to confuse them about the efficiency of their hired hands. They lost him, apparently because of random happenings. His luck was phenomenal!

One thing the type was really convinced was true was that "You can't beat luck!" He was apparently a little stupid and naive, but had luck on his side, and that would be damned scarey to them – while their own luck seemed to be holding out, at the same time.

That made it a very tricky balance that might change at any time.

There was a short wait for the hour to be up, then he went into the hotel and up to Dumas' room, where he collected the five thousand in twenties. He chatted about the great time he had last night for a few minutes, then said he would do his shopping as soon as they handled things at the bank. A quarter to four at the terminal. He'd be there with bells on – which he had to explain.

He got an idea, and grinned to himself.

They went to the bank, where Nito was known. Very well. Vonny had taken a few papers he gave her to the bank before it officially opened. It would mean a legal-looking account would be opened with an apparent deposit/transfer of five million pounds and change.

They met with a very stern, serious man, the vice president of the bank, to argue for about fifteen minutes, then a computer-generated form was filled in, notarized, and recorded. There was now an account, MSDfnd SA, in the bank, all legal and aboveboard. In three days, at 8:49AM, it would be available for use by any of the signatories. Until that moment, they had to make do with what they had.

Nito went shopping. Dumas and Suarez went their own way. He bought a good machete and scabbard, a leather belt, and a few items of clothing, then had a very good meal at the Ciudad de David, then walked around the town for awhile, until time to get his luggage from the hotel and meet Dumas and Saurez at the bus terminal. Nilsa was there, and asked him what was going on with the clown nose and bells on his shoes. Dumas and Suarez were aghast. He got the giggles.

"It's a joke. I used an old expression I learned in England, and made a joke from it for my friends."

He introduced Dumas and Suarez.

The bus was loading, so he was just getting on when Nando came to greet him and chat a minute. Dumas and Suarez were nervous and more than a little irritated by it.

Nito felt that the last thing they wanted was to be particularly noticed. He was making damned sure *everybody* noticed them. After all, how was he, the mark, to know they wanted to remain anonymous people in the background?

Vonny was sitting on the bench in front of the

bus. She grinned and giggled. She said something into the cell phone in her hand, and giggled again. The big black, who he'd "accidentally" managed to lose again at El Poderosa, was across at the open air restaurant. He looked mad as hell for some unfathomable reason.

The door boy from the bus said for him to get aboard. They were going. He suddenly looked surprised, started to say something, and mouthed "Nito Faraday?" Nito nodded, and said he was ready to get this show on the road!

The bus to Soloy was a bit crowded. Nito was asked to move from where he was seated, across from Dumas and Suarez, to a seat farther back, so a pregnant woman could sit close to the front. He said, "Why, certainly!" and shrugged at Dumas and Suarez. He moved back to a seat first in front of the rear seat, next to a middle-aged Indio man who was a little drunk. Dumas was turned around to see where he was seated, and he rolled his eyes and sat.

It was noisy. You couldn't hear anyone a seat away. The Indio said, "Yantoro, Nito!. I'm Balbino Green. I'm in a disguise you taught me at academy!" He didn't look up, and seemed to be dozing.

Balbino [Bino] had been a student when Nito taught a class in undercover surveillance and protection. He was about 24, but looked like he couldn't be less than forty five.

"From Buabidi? You're here for my case?"

"Yes. Silvio and Edmondo want to be sure you're safe, and I was the only one available, so they had to use me as last choice!"

They joked, neither one looking like they even knew the other was there.

Nito wondered what was going to happen now. Bino was a jokester, and knew he wanted to be noticed. It would make him a little bit safer. It would also make Dumas and Suarez' plans a little out of sync with what they predicted.

Just before Morito, where the bus turned to go to Soloy, a police truck pulled the bus over. Two officers with AK-47's came aboard and started checking everyone's ID. They as much as ignored Dumas, but gave Suarez a hard time, saying something had been changed on his cedula. The second officer came to stare suspiciously at Nito. He took a long time checking his passport, calling in on the radio twice. They checked his luggage, and asked what he was doing going onto the comarca. He acted like he was a little scared, and said he was on a vacation and wanted to see how the Indigenos lived.

They were by the luggage, and Dumas was standing nearby. "Are you that reporter from La Prenza who is giving the police here in Panamá a bad reputation by only reporting half of a story?"

Dumas' mouth fell open, and his eyes flew open wide.

"*Me*!? A reporter? For some Spanish magazine or something?! Are you quite *mad*!!??" Nito squealed.

The officer called in again, then looked sheepish, handed Nito his passport, and carefully repacked his maleta. "I'm most sorry, Sir! We are searching for a man who is suspected of working with the cartels in Colombia to dishonor the police here. His name, on his passport, the one we passed, was James Martin. He fits your description in many ways. I wish to apologize for any inconvenience!"

"Oh, I guess these things happen! Consider it forgotten! You have a job to do, and were doing it!"

They got back on the bus. Dumas shook his head. "This is a trip right through Hell!" he complained, as he took his seat. Suarez asked what happened, and he was explaining as Nito went back to his seat. Bino was giggling, which Nito was glad couldn't be seen by Dumas or Suarez, had they been looking.

"They called in your passport three times and Suarez' cedula twice! Sort of hard to stay anonymous, would you say?" Bino said.

Nito gave him the finger, and giggled, himself.

The bus then went on. Just before Soloy, an Indio boy, about eight years old, ran out in front of the bus, which screeched to a stop. The boy was laying on the road. Two local people ran out, and were working over the boy. Nito ran to the front of the bus, where the door boy grinned at him and hissed, "Not real!"

The boy sat up, and looked confused and dazed. Nito asked a man what was happening?

"It was an almost accident," he replied. "The bus hardly touched the boy, but it was enough to knock him down. Youth can be so careless!"

Nito went to look at the boy.

Eduardo? Nando's son? Eduardo winked at him. What now?

"I represent the council. I am Tomas Duarte. I must have everyone's cedula number for the report, in case there are questions you can answer. I am sure there will be none, because the driver was alert enough that there was no damage. Please present your cedula to Alena and myself, and we will allow you to proceed."

Most were still on the bus. A woman went aboard and started writing down cedula numbers. Tom grinned at Nito and said, "It would seem you can't go a kilometer without being recorded, doesn't it?

"What's going on? I'm not worth a tenth of all this!"

"Ever heard the name, 'Ponces?' *He* is!"

Nito thought. *What was the name of that Colombian who's involved in this, somehow? I think it was Ponces!*

"I think so. A connection?"

"He is a Colombian who is gathering funds to finance a little guerilla war in Venezuela. He has just been traced to a connection with the murders of two people near your home in Tula. Your companions are being used. Cruiz is in partnership with Ponces. We are trying to keep you safe until we can get some proof.

"Ponces is in Tula."

"Not such a simple little murder case, huh"

"Your part? Yes. Our part? No."

Nito got back on the bus. It took about four minutes to get everyone's ID recorded. Dumas and Suarez were looking very sick and very pissed.

They went on into Soloy. Nito noticed that Suarez kept trying to make a call on his cellular, but it apparently wasn't getting through. He checked his phone. There was a fair signal.

There was no signal at Quebrada Tula, as he knew. So!

The trio booked into the only rooms available. There was some kind of fiesta, the local schools marching for education. These people took advantage of any reason to have a fiesta!

Nito's room was comfortable, if not fancy. He was in back, away from the street. Dumas and

Suarez had a room with a balcony over the street, where the parade went on late into the night. Lots of drums! Lots of noise!

Just before they went to their rooms for the night, Dumas said, very sourly, "The trip wasn't *through* Hell! It's ended us up right in the middle of town in Hell!"

"Well, I'll stay optimistic! It will be worth it!" Nito exclaimed.

"I begin to wonder," Suarez replied, as sourly.

The fiesta lasted until a little after three thirty AM. They had to catch the Tula bus at five. There was noplace to get any breakfast, even coffee. Nito had slept well, but Dumas and Suarez looked like they would drop at any moment. A girl had brought him coffee and hojaldras at 4:15.

"Well! It's going to be a nice day! I can feel it!" Nito greeted Dumas and Suarez. "It's a good thing I don't need a lot of sleep, though. It wasn't easy to sleep, what with the noise."

"It was *impossible* to sleep!" Dumas cried. "I need ... *must* have ... some coffee!"

"There's noplace open, but there is a cart who might get here before we leave," the bus driver said. "I hope the road's open. There's a big tree that fell across it about thirty kilometers out. I think they should have time to clear the road before we get there."

Dumas groaned. Just as the bus was starting out, the coffee cart came, and the driver said three minutes to get coffee, then they had to be on the road. Dumas got three coffees and the last three empanadas. The coffee was just coffee, which Nito liked, but Dumas wanted sugar and Suarez wanted sugar and milk. They could take it black or not at all, so they took it black. The empanadas were a little greasy, but good.

There were only two others on the bus. The driver said the fiesta meant many would oversleep the dawn, but he had to run the route. There would be people waiting along the way.

They picked up a woman and child, then two men. The woman went all the way to Tula, but the men got off to go to work on a cattle ranch. Suarez and Dumas were as much as passed out in the back seat. Nito sat just behind the driver. There was no door boy on this bus.

"Nito, you are to find a way to speak with a man called Antonio Smith in Tula," the driver said, not looking around at him.

He didn't say anything more. Nito dozed a bit, but loved the scenery, so looked at it for most of the trip. The tree was moved, except for a few odd branches. They passed, and Nito asked if that was a setup.

"Yes, but to keep anyone from coming back from Tula last night." He warned Nito with his eyes to not talk. He managed to look at the two passengers in the mirror. They seemed asleep, but he couldn't be sure. "You don't know them?" Nito asked, very quietly. The driver nodded.

He sat back and looked at the scenery for awhile, then dozed, then they were at Quebrada Tula, a very small puebla in a paradise setting. They got off the bus and stretched, then walked around a bit to get past the stiffness of a bit of an uncomfortable, bumpy ride. It was a tosca [gravel and clay] road for a lot of the way, and just scraped off rock part. It was just past noon and getting darker. The driver announced that it would be raining soon, so find a dry spot for a couple of hours. He said they could get a meal at Ana's house, which was as close to a restaurant as they had.

He picked up the four people waiting for the bus and headed out.

Ana's house was the place they would stay the night. Nito said that, after that bus ride, he wasn't about to stay in that damned shed near Misty mountain, and he damned well wasn't about to ride a horse for another three or four hours – in the rain, yet!

Dumas and Suarez said they were going to look

around town for awhile. Nito said he was going to relax for a bit, then he would walk around a bit, himself.

As soon as they were away, he asked Ana where he could find Antonio Smith. She said to go to the little almacen. He was waiting.

He met with Tonio to learn Ponces was in the shack at Misty Mountain. There was a big black man there who had come from Soloy late last night. By helicopter. That meant big money backing. They would have the place surrounded, but it was up to Nito to protect himself as much as possible, or they would give themselves away. He gave Nito a .32 automatic pistol. It was small and easy to conceal.

Nito went out to walk around a little. The rain had stopped. He came across Dumas and Suarez by a little cabin near the stream. They had beer, so he had one, himself. As soon as they found a place where a woman would cook them dinner, if they bought the ingredients, for a dollar a plate. Dumas went to the almacen and bought some vegetables, rice, beans, and canned tuna. They had a really good meal, Gloria, the woman who cooked it, got her three dollars and a lot of vegetables, plus a sack of parotos [kidney beans] and several cans of tuna.

They went back to Ana's, where Nito got the

only room to himself, and Dumas and Suarez had hammocks on the porch. Just before they went to bed, Dumas said, "I think we should have stayed in David another night or two! Another night in Hell!"

It was a fairly nice dawn, but it would rain in a couple of hours, according to Ana. They got three horses from Edwin, the Indio who took care of them there. Antonio was cleaning the water tank, and two young children, six or eight years old, were helping with the feed and saddles and such. The children apparently didn't speak Spanish. They only knew the dialect.

Nito spoke dialect with them when Dumas and Suarez were arguing about some supplies that were supposed to be there, but weren't. He had been raised speaking Spanish, English, and dialect. These were raised the same, but that was known only on the comarca, where the schools his father built taught them. His mother found, while very young, that those languages became natural if the child was raised with all spoken from a very young age.

One of them carried some feed to pour into a trough very close to where Dumas and Suarez were talking. They ignored him. He soon was joined by the other boy, who brought another sack of feed, then he came back while the other boy poured and leveled the feed.

"They have a little radio thing they are talking to someone they call Estevez." the first boy reported. "They are having terrible luck. Everything is going wrong, and they are worried, because you seem to have nothing but good luck. They will be at the bodega in about four hours, so it can happen then.

"I couldn't hear what the other side said. Something about balanced and aimed."

All this while acting like he couldn't understand Nito, but they seemed to be sharing some kind of joke. Nito gave him one of the empanadas he'd bought at Ana's.

The other boy was coming back, and Dumas was checking the pack on his horse, while Suarez was taking a piss by a tree. The first boy went to talk with Antonio, and the second came to say that they wanted this to be finished before dark, and that the money was in the bank. They had a receipt.

He then went to help Antonio and the first boy, chewing on the empanada Nito gave him.

Nito went to where Dumas and Suarez were standing by the horses. "Well! Ready to go? I'm feeling *very* lucky today. Like when I won six hundred on the wheel, then heard that I had inherited several million pounds on the same day! I felt just like I do now!

"What's the package on my horse?"

"We will be making three trips, so we want to have some thing in the shed," Suarez replied. "We have packages on all three horses. They're backpacks, reinforced for the weight. We can wear them as we leave. It will mean acting like they are only ten pounds instead of sixty! We'll also have a few pounds that we will show Edmondo. Say about five pounds apiece.

"That will be sixty five pounds each. A total of a hundred ninety five pounds, at twelve ounces per pound, at two grand an ounce. Two thousand, three hundred forty ounces, at two grand per. Four million, six hundred eighty thousand dollars.

"Not bad for a week's work!"

Nito said he would have to agree with that!

They mounted up, and started riding along the trail. "Have you figured how we wait for the bus and get on without anyone knowing we have sixty pounds in our backpacks?" Nito asked.

Suarez laughed. "Why, just by complete fortunate accident, a friend from David will happen to be going back to David just then – and will take us with him, thereby saving us the bus fare!"

"Yeah! I've gone through the five grand, and

won't have the bus fare – until after nine tomorrow morning! Then we can buy our own luxury bus, like the musicians do!"

They all laughed. That started a bit of a joke session as they rode along. Dumas seemed to be thinking, then reined up, and said, "My god! I left the ... I forgot to ... we have to go back to Tula! We can't go to Misty Mountain until tomorrow! There won't be time today!"

"What?!" from Suarez.

"Well, it's not going anywhere, so one day isn't shit," Nito said. "I kind of like riding in the mountains! I think I might buy a horse ranch. Tula's sort of nice, so ... what the hell?"

"Let's stop and discuss ... what's going on?" Suarez asked.

"Remember Sr. Ponces, from Colombia? The one who's going to transport for us?" Dumas asked. "He has to be informed of things. He has to be where we can get it to him! I can't just call him up and say it's here!" He pointed to Nito [who seemed to be looking at something to the side] with his lips, and shook his head.

Nito dismounted and led the horse toward the little creek they were following. Dumas waited until he was a distance away, then said, in rapid Spanish [which they thought he didn't understand. He kept saying "Habla dispacio!"

when he talked to the natives, and didn't seem to understand half of what they were saying.], "Es importante que otras ver el es viviendo a la nueve!" ["It is important that others see he is alive at nine!"] Suarez looked shocked, and nodded. He rode off a little way, and behind some trees.

Nito grinned. Ponce and friend would have to be informed that they couldn't carry out their plan until tomorrow morning!

They headed back to Quebrada Tula. Suarez asked of no one, "What the hell else is going to fuck up this mess?"

They took their same accommodations when they got back to Tula. Antonio saw them, and raised an eyebrow at Nito, who smirked.

Later, he went to the little almacen, where he explained to one of the boys from the horse ranch what was happening.

It was a pleasant afternoon and night – for him. Dumas and Suarez were apprehensive, a little scared, and in rather foul mood.

Dumas made arrangements to use the horses about nine the following morning. Maybe they could get things back on track by then. He could hope!

They managed to get on the trail again at nine fifteen. Dumas seemed extremely nervous, while Suarez was mostly silent. Nito took a lot of pictures with his digital camera, stopping twice to take pictures of orchids. He had a large collection of the lower elevation types at his home in Cusapín, as well as a great variety of the types found at higher elevations at Quebrada Tule. He remembered how the nutty botanist friend of his father had planted hundreds of different species at both places.

He wondered if Dave had a picture of that very same plant, and if it was one that was found nowhere else. It was certainly odd, and one he'd never seen. It could be a natural hybrid, basically *Scaphyglottis* and/or *Epidendrum*.

Weird. Thinking about an orchid classification while he was being taken to a place where they planned to kill him!

They came to the shed at a few minutes before four o'clock. Nito noted that some trees were cut above it, where it sat at the bottom of a sharp cleft. He looked up, and saw a very large boulder near the top of the cleft.

So. He was to be in the shed, the boulder was to be dislodged, and he would be crushed. Ooooh how sad!

He moved away from Dumas and Saurez and lower down the cleft to take a picture of the shed and the boulder, Dumas asked what that was for.

"I want a picture of where I stayed for the album. It is sort of nice. Tranquil mountain hut sort of thing."

"Oh. Want to go to the lode now, or rest up a bit?"

"I want to relax for awhile, and change clothes.

"I bought a hammock with mosquito netting, but there don't seem to be any mosquitoes up here."

"There are flies that carry parasites. That's why we stay in the closed shed. That, and it gets cold before dawn," Suarez said. "There are tigers, but it's rare for them to attack anyone.

"You can bathe in the stream, but you might find the water to be cold.

"I think I'll look around. As silly as it may seem, I think there's some gold in the stream. I want to go a little lower to see."

"I'll go with you. I don't know about gold, but I'm sure there's jade. There are a few little pieces right here!" He picked up a green rock. "It *is* silly! We come for a few million in platinum and pick up fifteen dollars worth of jade! I'm greedy, and admit it!"

Nito said he would bathe, then rest in the shed. They could break out some food later. They all agreed, and Dumas and Suarez went to beside the stream and moved downward. Nito knew they wanted to use the radio, and maybe meet with Ponces.

Was the big black man the same one from David?

Probably. He came by chopper. He was probably insurance if the boulder didn't work.

Was Antonio watching all this?

He couldn't strip to bathe. That would give his disguise away.

He went to the stream, where he splashed water on his face, and jumped back. It really was cold at this altitude. It would be logical that he would wash his face and hands and say, "No way!" to a full bath.

He puttered around for long enough that Dumas and friends would be getting antsy, then went into the shed. There was a little window in back, and a thick cedar tree hiding it from view. He was barely able to get out. It was small, but he managed. He went through the cedar branches and off to the side, where he slid into a little crevice.

There was a rumbling sound from above, and the boulder came down directly onto the shed, then rolled on to the stream, barely missing Suarez, but hitting Dumas solidly. Suarez has a bright gleam in his eyes. He sat on a log and lit a cigarette.

"Au revoir!" Nito hissed. Dumas should have known better than to be that close to the boulder's path.

After about ten minutes, the big black and a brutish Latino thug type came from the forest above, and down to Suarez.

"Perfect!" Suarez said. "Both of my poooor dear partners had an accident, and all I'm left with is the five million dollars in the bank! Oh, woe is me!" He giggled. "Oh, I wish I had a phone that worked here, so I could call someone to help me in my time of grief!"

They all three laughed.

"Nito! We have it all! Come on out!" Antonio called, as he came strolling, with Nando, from the path to Tula.

Nito came out of the crevice and down to them. The black suddenly grabbed a machete and went for Antonio. Nito had the .32 in his hand, expecting something such, and shot him before he reached Antonio. Nando was drawing his own pistol, and covered Ponces. Suarez ran into the jungle.

"There's nowhere to go, so you might as well come on back!" Nando called. "Every indigeno on the comarca will be looking for you!"

Ponces was hunched in an attack position, but saw he was covered by two pistols, so put his hands on his head.

"I'm unarmed! I will come with my hands in sight!" Suarez called, and came back.

"Milcare Suarez M., I place you under arrest on charges of murder, first degree, of two persons, and suspicion of complicity in other murders," Nito said, showing his badge. "If you resist or try to flee, you will be shot.

"Nando, do you have anyone to carry those two back to Tula?"

"No. We can pack them on the horses and take them back. We have all of it, since David, here, David, Soloy, and Quebrada Tula, on video.

"I think, just perhaps, we have put a little stumbling block on a guerrilla revolution scheme."

"And this was done by the Ngobe, not the Panamanian police!" Antonio stated, emphatically.

They put the bodies on the horses and headed back to Quebrada Tula.

Clintonito Faraday laid back in the hammock. His son came to hand him the guanabana chicha, and climb into the hammock with him.

"Dad, what happened to the platinum there?"

"So far as I know, it's still there. You can get it next time we're at Tula, if you want it."

"Maybe a little piece, just for a memory of what my Dad did. You're like Grandpops!"

"That would be a great legacy to leave."

They laid in silence for a few minutes, then, "Dad? You know Cecilio?"

"Cecilio? Your friend at the village?"

"Yes."

"What?"

"He's gay, and he wants to be with me for sex."

"Do you want that?"

"Well, from my end of the stick, maybe. For him. I'm not sure. I do like him, as a friend."

"It's up too you. It has to be understood that you aren't interested in being on the other end of the deal."

"He knows that. It's what he wants, but he wants me to love him, and I do, in a way, as a friend, but not that way, and I'm not *in* love with him."

"You mean make love? How far? It's up to you, but only if you both understand the other, and agree."

"Just to lay together like we are now. The sex would be one way. I think it's kind of nice to lay together, but I couldn't get into kissing and all that."

"He knows that?"

"Yeah."

"If it's decided who does what and why, why ask me? It's only between you two."

"Because you always said Grandpops went crazy when you asked him things like that. I was trying to get to you!" He laughed.

Nito laughed, in return. "It does sort of bother me a little, but I'm like him. I have to be the 'Oh? Really" Did you like it?' one now!"

"It was a real question, sort of."

"And a real answer – sort of!"

They hugged tightly.

After awhile, Nito asked how the vegetable garden was doing. Had the worm problem been solved?

Yes. There would be a lot of zucchini for the next few weeks, and all the neighbors knew to come get what they could use. There were a lot of recipes that they used it with, including sopa de pollo, or just breaded and fried in garlic butter. Zucchini, tomatoes, and onion in a stew was delicious!

That was another thing his father taught them. The whole village loved zucchini. He supplied it, and they would supply other things. They shared on the comarca. No one went without the important things in life. That included the very real love of the family and friends.

C. D. Moulton's works are available on most major outlets as printed or e-books. CD writes the CD Grimes, PI, mysteries, the Det. Lt. Nick Storie mysteries, the Clint Faraday mysteries, the Flight of the Maita science fiction series, books on orchid culture and many others of many types. Mystery, adventure, intrigue, science fiction, humor, fantasy, paranormal, mild erotica, and factual.

* 9 7 9 8 2 2 3 5 3 2 8 5 9 *